JOHN CONSTANTINE, HELLBLAZER: S T A T I O N S   O F   T H E   C R O S S

JOHN CONSTANTINE, HELLBLAZER:
STATIONS OF THE CROSS

Mike Carey
Writer

Leonardo Manco
Chris Brunner
Marcelo Frusin
Steve Dillon
Artists

Lee Loughridge
Colorist

Clem Robins
Letterer

Tim Bradstreet
Original Series Covers

JOHN CONSTANTINE, HELLBLAZER: STATIONS OF THE CROSS

Published by DC Comics. Cover and compilation copyright ©
2006 DC Comics. All Rights Reserved.

DC Comics, 1700 Broadway, New York, NY 10019
A Warner Bros. Entertainment Company
Printed in Canada. First Printing.

ISBN: 1-4012-1002-3
ISBN 13: 978-1-4012-1002-1

Cover illustration by Tim Bradstreet.
Logo design by Nessim Higson.

I HAVEN'T FORGOTTEN-- I WAS--I WAS *JOKING* WITH HER.

YOU'VE TAKEN SOME KIND OF *WOUND* TO THE THROAT. YOU'RE PROBABLY IN *SHOCK.*

FORGETTING YOUR *NAME* ISN'T A GOOD SIGN.

MY NAME'S-- *SUMNER.*

MY NAME'S LEO SUMNER.

WELL I DON'T THINK YOU'RE READY TO GO BACK OUT ON THE *STREET,* LEO.

I THINK YOU SHOULD LET A *DOCTOR* TAKE A LOOK AT YOU.

COME ON, MR. SUMNER.

WELL, NO. I'VE GOT TO--

BELIEVE ME, YOU'LL *THANK* US FOR THIS IN THE MORNING.

NAME: LEO SUMNER
ADDRESS: ✓
PHONE NUMBER: ✓
ETIOLOGY:
MEDICATION:
PRESENTING WITH: CONFUSION, MEMORY LOSS, SLURRED SPEECH
...CESS TO: PSYCH UNIT, WARD 24, Dr. BRADSHAW

10·8

'SCUSE ME.

WE'LL GET TO YOU AS SOON AS WE *CAN*, SIR.

YOU CAN SEE WHAT WE'RE *DEALING* WITH HERE.

NO, IT'S OKAY. I'M JUST WAITING TO PICK SOMEONE *UP*.

ONLY-- I THOUGHT THAT MIGHT HAVE BEEN HIM.

NOT LIKELY. BUT IF IT IS YOU'LL HAVE TO TALK TO DR. BRADSHAW IN THE *PSYCHIATRIC* UNIT.

WARD 24. WE'RE KEEPING THE PATIENT IN FOR *OBSERVATION*.

THANKS.

AND YOU'RE *RIGHT* BY THE WAY...

...YOUR DAD *WAS* RAPING YOUR KID SISTER.

TOO BAD YOU DIDN'T TELL ANYONE WHILE IT COULD'VE DONE SOME *GOOD*.

DON'T KNOW WHY I PANICKED BACK THERE.

WHY I COULDN'T JUST ADMIT THAT-- I'VE DROPPED THE BALL. *LOST* MYSELF.

COME ALONG IN PLEASE.

COME ALONG *IN*, LEO. MY NAME'S MILES BRADSHAW.

I'M A PSYCHIATRIST. AND YOU'RE HERE BECAUSE WE THINK SOME OF THE HELP YOU NEED MIGHT BE *PSYCHIATRIC* HELP.

SO I'M GOING TO ASK YOU SOME QUESTIONS, AND I'M GOING TO TRY TO FORM AN *OPINION* ABOUT WHAT HAPPENED TO YOU, OKAY?

OKAY.

I SUPPOSE.

LITTLE·NEMO

WHERE ARE YOU *FROM*, LEO?

WHERE AM I--?

WHERE WERE YOU *BORN*, I MEAN? AND WHERE ARE YOU LIVING NOW?

I'M FROM HERE, I SUPPOSE.

AND THIS IS WHERE I LIVE. SOMEWHERE *NEAR* HERE.

WELL, THIS IS A BIT OF A *MESS*, ISN'T IT?

YOU'LL HAVE TO TELL ME IF IT *HURTS*, ALL RIGHT?

ALL RIGHT.

AND IF IT HURTS I'LL *STOP* AND JUST STEEP THE BANDAGES.

THAT'S A GOOD GIRL.

JUST *ONE* MORE AND THEN WE'RE DONE.

HOW DID YOU GET THIS WAY, ROSE?

WHERE WAS THE FIRE?

IN HER

WHERE'S *YOURS?*

I WANT TO KNOW WHO YOU *ARE*, MATEY.

I WANT TO KNOW WHY I DON'T *KNOW* YOU. I KNOW EVERYBODY ELSE.

THAT *WOMAN* OVER THERE. THE WEST INDIAN. GOT SIX KIDS, SHE HAS.

AND SHE'S SHIT SCARED HUBBY WILL TWIG THAT NUMBER SIX ISN'T *HIS*.

AND THE BLOKE WITH THE *WALKMAN*--HE'S OFF HIS CHUMP.

THINKS HE'S BEEN CHOSEN TO SAVE THE WORLD. ONLY HE'S GOT TO *WAIT* UNTIL HIS ORDERS COME THROUGH.

BUT YOU-- YOU'RE AN INTERNATIONAL MAN OF BLOODY *MYSTERY*.

A RIDDLE WRAPPED IN A *MYSTERY* INSIDE OF FUCK ALL.

SO WHAT'S THE *STORY*?

AND IT BETTER BE *FULL* OF HUMAN INTEREST.

GUUUH! PLEASE! I DON'T *KNOW*! I DON'T KNOW WHO I AM!

YOU'RE SAFE.

YOU'RE PERFECTLY, ABSOLUTELY SAFE.

YOU'RE IN A PLACE WHERE NOTHING CAN HURT YOU. AND YOU CAN GO BACK TO THAT PLACE ANY TIME YOU WANT TO.

ANY TIME YOU FEEL UNHAPPY OR AFRAID.

NOW I WANT YOU TO THINK BACK. FAR, FAR BACK. AS FAR AS YOU CAN GO.

ARE YOU THERE? HAVE YOU DONE THAT?

YES.

GOOD. WHERE ARE YOU NOW?

WHAT ARE YOU SEEING?

THE MIST ON THE RIVER.

THIS MORNING.

LET'S COME TO THE RIVER FROM THE OTHER SIDE.

GO **BACK** FROM THE RIVER. BACK TO WHERE YOU WERE BEFORE THAT.

NOWHERE-- BEFORE.

THEN THINK OF A **VOICE**. A FACE. A NAME.

ANYTHING THAT YOU'VE **KEPT** FROM THAT TIME BEFORE. NO MATTER HOW SMALL.

NO? THEN I'LL GIVE **YOU** A NAME.

AND I WANT YOU TO TELL ME WHAT **MEMORIES** GO WITH IT. ARE YOU READY?

JOHN.

CONSTANTINE.

NNNNNNNNN!

OKAY, *REST* NOW. GO BACK TO THAT PLACE. THAT *SAFE* PLACE.

THAT'S WHERE YOU *ARE* NOW. IN THAT SAFE PLACE.

HEY! YOU CAN'T COME IN *HERE*, LOVE.

I'M WORKING.

I KNOW.

THEN LET'S PUT YOU BACK IN YOUR--

HFFFF! YOU'RE A LOT HEAVIER THAN YOU *LOOK*.

YOU WON'T *GET* HIM THERE.

A FEW IMAGES. A FEW *GHOSTS* OF SPENT EMOTIONS. THAT'S ALL YOU CAN GIVE HIM.

BUT IT'S STILL TOO *MUCH*.

MUM! DAD! THAT'S THE LAST OF THE CASES.

WHAT'S KEEPING YOU?

OH, GREAT.

I TOLD YOU, CHAS! I TOLD YOU A HUNDRED BLOODY TIMES!

RENEE, I DON'T WANT TO ARGUE ABOUT IT, OKAY?

THEN JUST READ IT.

READ IT AND BLOODY WEEP?

THE SUNDAY TIMES
HOSPITAL SLAYING: MANHUNT

Police began a nationwide manhunt yesterday for a former punk rock star, wanted for questioning in relation to a bloody slaying at Paddington's Praed Street Hospital.

Doctor Miles Bradshaw, 42, a clinical psychologist, was found dead by his own staff nurse at the end of an eight-hour shift during which he had seen upwards of twenty patients. He had been extensively mutilated either before or just after death.

Janet Edwards, 25, who found the body, has been

sent home on extended sick leave. "I've been a nurse seven years", she said, "but I've never in all my days seen anything like this".

Police are particularly keen to interview John Constantine, a former rock star and self-confessed black magician. Constantine had been admitted to the hospital claiming memory loss, but his identity was soon established by the use of the home office's centralised missing persons database

"It seems likely that John Constantine was the last

person to see Doctor Bradshaw alive", said Detective Sergeant Walter Melly, of the Met's Serious Crimes Unit. "We think he may have information vital to the success of this inquiry".

However, he cautioned members of the public against approaching Constantine themselves.

"He was after all in a psychiatric unit. There's no telling what state of mind he may be in".

Drunk BA captain and

BRITIS

31

STILL.

AT LEAST THE **RAIN'S** STOPPED, eh?

PITY I COULDN'T FIND A BETTER **TRUCK,** THOUGH.

I MAY BE **STARVING,** BUT I'M NOT EATING THESE BASTARD THINGS ON A BET.

AND ME STILL A COUPLE OF **DEGREES** AWAY FROM HYPOTHERMIA.

LONG PIG. DOESN'T THAT MEAN HUMAN **FLESH?** MEAT MADE OUT OF **PEOPLE?**

THINGS ARE LOOKING **UP.**

HOW DID I **KNOW** THAT?

I'VE GOT A **HEAD** FULL OF MONSTERS.

AND I DON'T EVEN KNOW THEIR **NAMES.**

I'M JUST DRIFTING INTO A *DOZE* WHEN WE STOP.

DOOR SLAMS. FOOTSTEPS *CRUNCH* OVER GRAVEL.

THEN SILENCE.

PROBABLY A GOOD TIME TO MAKE A *MOVE*.

BEFORE SONNY JIM DECIDES TO CHECK ON THE PIG BYPRODUCTS.

HE'S LEFT THE CAB OPEN. AND THAT'S HIS *JACKET* LYING ON THE SEAT.

I STAND THERE FOR A MINUTE OR SO, LIKE A KID OUTSIDE A *CONFESSIONAL*.

BUT HOW FAR WILL I GET IN A GREEN *TARPAULIN?* I TELL MYSELF I'LL FIND SOME WAY TO PAY HIM *BACK*.

AND I LEAVE HIM HIS *CREDIT* CARDS.

DESPERATE *SITUATIONS*, AND ALL THAT.

BUT MAYBE I WAS *ALWAYS* LIKE THIS.

MAYBE I ALWAYS FOUND THE *EXCUSE* I NEEDED TO SCREW SOME POOR BASTARD OVER.

NO, BUT THAT STUFF I TOOK IN THE LOCKUP-- I'VE *STILL* GOT IT IN MY SYSTEM.

I THINK I CAN FIND HIM. JUST ANCHOR ME, OKAY?

CLIFTONVILLE
SEAFRONT PAVILION

WHERE DOES HE *LIVE*, THEN, THIS JOHN BLOKE?

WHERE DOES HE *GO* WHEN HE'S CAUGHT IN THE RAIN?

I MUST HAVE FRIENDS. FAMILY.

A MEAL ON A TABLE *WAITING* FOR ME SOMEWHERE.

BUT THOSE *THINGS* I SAW WHEN I WAS HYPNOTIZED--BITS OF MY *LIFE*.

FUCKING *NIGHTMARES*.

MAYBE IT'S BETTER NOT TO *KNOW*.

"OPEN APRIL TO OCTOBER"

AND ANYWAY--

--GOD ALWAYS *PROVIDES*.

TCHUNG

TCHUNG
TCHUNG

OY! YOU!

WHAT YOU WANNA GO USING THE **MACHINES** FOR? SOME BUGGER WILL 'EAR THE RACKET AND **CLOCK** US.

ARE YOU **THICK** OR SOMETHING?

HERE. DON'T I **KNOW** YOU?

NO. DEFINITELY **NOT.** I'VE NEVER--

HEATHROW. TERMINAL 3. TWO WEEKS AGO. YOU BUNGED ME A **FIVER.**

DON'T YOU **WORRY,** MATE. DON'T YOU **BLOODY** WORRY.

YOU'VE FALLEN ON YOUR **FEET** THIS TIME. **JINX'LL** TAKE CARE OF YOU.

ALMOST *THERE*, NOW.

EVERYONE *HAPPY* IN THE BACK?

LOOK, TRISH--IT'S THE *SEA*.

WHERE ARE THE *WHALES?*

WELL--I'M SURE THEY'RE HANGING AROUND SOME-WHERE. SWIMMING ALONG THE *BOTTOM*, MAYBE.

I'LL DROP YOU LOT IN FRONT OF THE *HOTEL*, THEN I'LL GO AND PARK UP, YEAH?

IT'S *THERE*, CHAS. YOU'RE GOING TO DRIVE PAST IT.

YEAH. WELL.

I'LL BRING THE CASES UP *MESELF*, THEN.

D'YOU FANCY ANY *ICE CREAM*, FISHFACE?

RABBIT'S EARS! RABBIT'S EARS, GRANDAD!

IT'S NEAR ON *DINNER* TIME. YOU CAN HAVE ONE AFTER.

THE CHALK *CLIFFS* THAT HAVE ALWAYS SAID "HOME" TO ENGLAND'S SAILORS.

THINK *HE* MUST HAVE COME HERE ONCE. A LONG TIME AGO.

BECAUSE THE SIGHT OF IT MEANS SOMETHING TO *ME*.

THE *UNDERTOW* EATING THEM AWAY ONE ATOM AT A TIME.

A MILLION *SEAGULLS* HANGING AROUND TO SEE HOW IT TURNS *OUT*.

JOHN CONSTANTINE WOZ 'ERE.

BUT HE'S NOT HERE *NOW*.

THE JACKET'S STILL GOT JINX ALL OVER IT. JINX'S *EBB-TIDE*. STIFF, DRY, MORE BROWN THAN RED.

SO WHAT DO YOU *DO* ABOUT THAT?

WHAT DO YOU FUCKING *DO*?

YEAH. YOU FALL BACK ON THE *DEFAULT* OPTION, DON'T YOU, MATE?

YOU WALK *AWAY*.

I KNOW WHAT YOU'RE **THINKING**, CHARLES.

YOU DON'T **MIND** ME CALLING YOU CHARLES, DO YOU? I DON'T FEEL I KNOW YOU WELL ENOUGH FOR CHAS. YET.

T-HINK

YOU'RE THINKING "HANDCUFFS? LEG RESTRAINTS? SIDE BATON?

"WERE YOU A **POLICEMAN** AT ANY TIME, MISTER GILL? OR A **SQUADDIE?**"

WELL I **WAS**, CHARLES. I WAS BOTH OF THOSE THINGS.

BUT MOST OF THIS KIT IS **MAIL** ORDER-- SO YOU GOT TO THE RIGHT PLACE BY THE WRONG **ROAD**. FUNNY, EH?

"YOUR BOLLOCKS IN HIS **POCKET**," SHE SAID. DIDN'T SHE?

AND THE LITTLE GIRL ASKED WHAT **BOLLOCKS** ARE. HEH!

GWRRRRRGHH!

NO, NO, CHARLES. I'LL TAKE GOOD **CARE** OF HER.

SHE'S ONLY COMING WITH ME TO MAKE SURE THE **REST** OF YOU BEHAVE WHILE I'M GONE.

PRETTY **CLOSE,** WHATEVER IT IS.

THE WRONG **COLOR** TO BE A SEARCHLIGHT.

NO SIRENS. NO RADIO CRACKLE. **THAT'S** GOOD, ANYWAY.

--MUSIC?

JUST A BUZZ OF **VOICES,** AND--

MEANING *WHAT*, EXACTLY? SPELL IT OUT FOR ME.

YOUR *PAST* LIFE. YOUR MEMORIES.

SWEAR YOURSELF INTO MY *SERVICE* FOR ONE DAY ONLY, AND I'LL GIVE THEM *BACK* TO YOU.

GILL IS COMING FOR YOU. THE *REAL* JOHN CONSTANTINE WOULD CHEW HIM UP AND SHIT HIM OUT.

BUT AS YOU ARE *NOW*? I WONDER...

WELL, FUCK.

THAT'S *MY* APPETITE GONE.

THIS WAS HIS LIFE, WASN'T IT? HE'D HAVE BEEN RIGHT AT HOME HERE.

WHY IN THE NAME OF *CHRIST* WOULD YOU THINK I'D WANT THAT BACK?

DON'T GET *UP.*

I CAN SEE *MYSELF* OUT.

MAKE IT TO THE *DOOR* WITHOUT LOOKING BACK.

WHEN I'VE CLOSED IT *BEHIND* ME I'LL RUN AND HIDE AND I'LL BE SOMEONE *ELSE*.

THIS ISN'T MY--

WHUK!

LOST YOU FOR A MOMENT, JOHN. SIGNAL GLITCH.

FLOCK OF *SEAGULLS* OR SOMETHING.

BUT YOU'RE HERE *NOW*.

THAT'S ALL THAT *MATTERS*.

NRRGHHHH!

IT'S OKAY! IT'S-- OKAY.

YOUR KID'S STILL *ALIVE.* SHE'S CAUGHT IN THE--IN THE PIGEON NETS. BUT I CAN'T UNTIE YOU.

I--I'VE GOT TO *GO,* RIGHT? I'LL MAKE SURE SOMEONE FINDS YOU, BUT I CAN'T--

HE MADE ME *DO* IT. HE FUCKING *MADE* ME--

OH GOD.

CLANG
CLANG
CLANG
CLANG

AND THE SUN COMES UP *ANYWAY.*

LIKE IT *ALWAYS* DOES.

THEY'LL TELL YOU IT'S THE **COLD.**

BUT IT'S **NOT** THE COLD.

IT'S NOT EVEN THE **DAMP,** ALTHOUGH THE DAMP GETS INTO **EVERYTHING.**

GIVES YOUR SLEEPING BAG THE RAZOR-EDGED **STINK** OF A COMPOST HEAP.

MAKES **FUNGUS** SPROUT BETWEEN YOUR TOES LIKE WHITE MEASLES.

AND THE SADISTIC COPPERS. AND THE LATE-NIGHT PSYCHOS. AND THE **PEDO** CARE ASSISTANTS AT THE SHELTER COMING ON TO YOU. IT'S NOT **ANY** OF THAT.

THREE MONTHS OUT FROM RHONDDA, AN OLD **HAND** IN LONDON NOW, YOU TAKE ALL THAT FOR GRANTED.

NO, THE **WORST** THING IS HAVING TO WATCH ALL THESE PEOPLE GOING PAST. THE ONES WITH MONEY TO **BUY** STUFF.

A SIT-DOWN **MEAL.**

A **HOTEL** ROOM.

A TICKET **HOME.**

ON A WET DAY, THE **UNDER-GROUND'S** A BETTER PITCH THAN OXFORD STREET.

BUT THE **CROATIANS** RUN MUM-AND-BABY TEAMS IN MOST OF THE WEST END STATIONS, AND YOU DON'T WANT TO RISK GETTING INTO A FIGHT WITH--

HI.

YOU'RE *HUGHIE*, AREN'T YOU?

NO.

YES YOU ARE. WE KNOW *EVERYONE* ON THE STREET.

WE *KNOW* EVERYONE BECAUSE WE *LOVE* EVERYONE.

I'M SUZIE. AND THIS IS MARGARET.

HUGHIE, WE'VE GOT THIS CHURCH *HALL* AROUND THE BACK OF CHARLOTTE STREET.

WE'RE SERVING SOUP AND *CHICKEN*. AND HOT COFFEE.

WE'VE GOT *BEDS*, TOO. YOU MIGHT HAVE TO SHARE A ROOM, BUT WE ALL MAKE A *PROMISE* TO SHARE EVERYTHING WE'VE GOT.

WON'T YOU COME AND *SHARE* WITH US, HUGHIE?

AND YOU TAKE UP YOUR BED AND *WALK*, LIKE JESUS TOLD THE LEPERS.

BECAUSE THREE MONTHS OUT FROM RHONDDA, WITH A DRY COUGH AND A *HEROIN* HUNGER AND CHRIST KNOWS *WHAT* INCUBATING IN YOUR SAD, SLOW BLOOD--

--YOU KNOW THAT A TICKET *HOME* IS IMPOSSIBLE.

YOU HAVE BEEN JUDGED AND GOD LOVES YOU

SO YOU'LL TAKE A TICKET TO *ANYWHERE*.

--PEOPLE EVERYWHERE, ASKING THE WRONG *QUESTIONS* OF GOD.

ASKING WHEN HE WILL COME DOWN, AND VISIT HIS *JUSTICE* ON THE SINNERS OF THIS WORLD.

WHEN THE GREAT *BEAST* WALKED THROUGH OUR CITIES, AND OUR HEARTS, DIDN'T WE *SEE* GOD'S JUSTICE?

DIDN'T WE SEE BABYLON TREMBLE TO ITS *BASE,* AS WE WERE PROMISED?

DON'T WORRY, HUGHIE, WE'LL GET THESE *DRY* FOR YOU.

THE PROPHET WILL WANT TO *WELCOME* YOU.

WHAT, I'VE GOT TO SAY I SAW BABYLON *TREMBLE* BEFORE I CAN HAVE ANY CHICKEN?

OH, THAT'S NOT THE *PROPHET,* SILLY. THAT'S JUST TERRY.

COME ON.

WE HAVE ALREADY BEEN JUDGED, AND GOD *LOVES* US.

WE KNOW HE LOVES US BECAUSE WE'RE STILL ALIVE!

A NEW **DISCIPLE**, SAVIOUR.

SHOULD WE GIVE HIM SOMETHING TO **EAT** FIRST, OR--

BRING HIM **IN**.

JUST BE **YOUR-SELF**, HUGHIE, AND YOU'LL BE FINE.

WE'LL SEE YOU **LATER**, IN THE KITCHEN.

AND MAYBE IN THE **DORMITORY**.

...N, ...E THE ...

...ETTER ...OCK IT, ...TOO.

SALVATION IS A VERY **PRIVATE** THING.

BLOODY HELL! I THINK THIS ONE'S *DEAD.*

MMNUH! WHA--?

NO HE AIN'T. HE JUST *SMELLS* LIKE IT. *HUR HUR HURR.*

COME ON, BLONDIE. NINE O'CLOCK, INNIT. YOU'RE *BUGGERED* IF YOU STAY 'ERE.

SHOP-KEEPERS CLUB TOGETHER FOR A *WATER* TRUCK. THEY HOSE THIS PLACE WITH *DETTOX* EVERY NIGHT.

SO NOBODY CAN KIP *DOWN* 'ERE, SEE?

SO-- WHERE *DO* YOU KIP DOWN? IF YOU DON'T MIND ME ASKING?

THAT'S *MY* BUSINESS, INNIT?

YOU JUST SOD *OFF.*

YOU TRY TO DO A BLOKE A *FAVOR,* AND HE'S AFTER YOUR BLEEDING ARSE.

'S ALWAYS THE FUCKING *SAME.*

HELLO, JOHN.

WE DO HAVE SOME *FUN* TOGETHER, DON'T WE?

"THE SOUL AS *PRODUCT*. THE BODY AS *PACKAGING*.

"CELESTIAL *ECONOMICS*. YOU SEE? YOU SEE?"

NO. LOOK, THOSE GIRLS SAID THERE WAS *FOOD*--

AND THERE *IS*. OH YES.

THE *TRUTH* IS FOOD. FOOD FOR THE *SOUL*.

TRUTH IS, I TRY TO *CONTROL* MYSELF. I MANAGE. *MOST* OF THE TIME.

BUT TODAY'S BEEN A BAD DAY.

HI THERE.

YOU'RE *HURT.* CAN WE *HELP* YOU?

NO! NO, I'M *FINE.* THANKS.

WE KNOW A PLACE WHERE YOU CAN GET A *BATH.* AND A BANDAGE FOR THAT CUT.

SOMETHING TO *EAT,* TOO, IF YOU'RE HUNGRY.

I'M *NOT* HUNGRY! PLEASE, JUST GO AWAY!

IT'S NOT SAFE TO BE NEAR ME. I *MEAN* IT!

BROTHER, YOUR SOUL IS *TROUBLED*.

I THINK IT'S BEEN A LONG TIME SINCE YOU KNEW ANY *PEACE*.

THEN *GIVE* ME SOME. CAN'T YOU TAKE A BLOODY--

WE KNOW A MAN WHO CAN TAKE YOUR BURDEN *AWAY* FROM YOU.

A PROPHET. A *SAVIOUR*.

HE'LL *SEE* YOUR PAIN AND HE'LL KNOW HOW TO *HEAL* IT.

AND IT'S NOT AS IF YOU'VE GOT ANYTHING TO *LOSE*.

IS IT?

CHRIIIIST!

IT'S JUST TINCTURE OF *IODINE*, FRIEND.

I'VE GOT TO CLEAN THE *CUTS*.

SORRY. IT STINGS. AND I DIDN'T SEE IT *COMING*.

THIS IS AN IMPRESSIVE SORT OF *SETUP*, ISN'T IT?

BACK OF OXFORD STREET. MUST BE A MILLION QUID PER CUBIC *INCH* OR SOMETHING.

PEOPLE WHO JOIN THE CHURCH GIVE EVERYTHING THEY'VE *GOT* TO THE PROPHET.

WE BOUGHT THE BUILDINGS ON EITHER *SIDE*, TOO. KNOCKED THEM ALL TOGETHER. WE'VE GOT PLENTY OF ROOM TO *EXPAND*.

SAVIOUR--

RIGHT. I'LL LEAVE YOU TO IT, THEN. THE DRESSING'S *WATERPROOF.*

SO YOU CAN HAVE A *SHOWER* NEXT DOOR, AND THEN COME IN TO THE SERVICE. I'LL GIVE YOU SOME *SUPPER* AFTERWARDS.

THE PROPHET'S ABOUT TO SPEAK.

HE SAYS HE'LL *RECEIVE* YOU IN FRONT OF EVERYONE. COME ON!

I CAN'T *STAY*. SORRY. I'M A MUSLIM. I PROBABLY SHOULD'VE *TOLD* YOU.

THE DOORS ARE *LOCKED.* NOBODY COMES IN OR GOES OUT DURING A SERVICE.

YOU DON'T *HAVE* TO TAKE OUR CHARITY--BUT YOU DO HAVE TO STAY UNTIL THE PROPHET HAS FINISHED *SPEAKING.*

JOHN, YOU DON'T UNDERSTAND HOW *LUCKY* YOU ARE.

HE DOESN'T *DO* THIS MUCH ANYMORE. JUST COME AND LISTEN TO HIM. PLEASE.

I'LL *STAY* WITH YOU. I PROMISE.

JUST LISTEN TO HIM SPEAK. IT'S A MESSAGE FOR *EVERYONE.*

THE *MASKS* OF GOD. THE PIECES OF GOD THAT ARE *HIDDEN* IN EACH ONE OF US.

THAT LONG TO BE *CONJOINED* AGAIN WHEN WE TOUCH THE TRUE GODHEAD.

"THEY SAY FAITH CAN MOVE *MOUNTAINS.*

"IN *MY* EXPERIENCE? NO. NEVER SEEN IT HAPPEN.

"*LIES* ARE MORE MY THING, ANYWAY.

"FUCK *MOUNTAINS.* WITH A GOOD LIE, YOU CAN MOVE *PEOPLE* AROUND.

"A LOT MORE FLEXIBLE, YEAH?

"A LOT MORE *USEFUL.*"

SO HERE WE ARE *AGAIN,* JOHN. JUST LIKE OLD TIMES.

EXCEPT THAT I'M TALKING AND *YOU'RE* LISTENING.

"THE **BONE ABACUS.** A WAY OF TALKING TO THE DEAD-- **COMPELLING** THE DEAD--

"--USING THEIR PHYSICAL **REMAINS** AS THE CONDUIT. IT WAS **PERFECT.** IT WAS FINALLY FUCKING **PERFECT.**

"BUT THEN **ANOTHER** CONSTANTINE STUCK HER BLOODY SNOUT IN.

"SET FREE ONE OF THE SOULS, AND WRECKED THE **BALANCE.**

"I'M GOING TO KILL **HER** TOO. I SHOULD HAVE DONE IT RIGHT THERE.

"BUT AT THE TIME IT WAS ALL I COULD DO TO GET AWAY WITH MY FUCKING **LIFE.**"

AND THEN LATER I REALIZED THAT I'D GOTTEN AWAY WITH A LITTLE **MORE** THAN THAT.

THE SOULS FROM THE ABACUS. TRYING TO FIND THEIR WAY **HOME.**

BUT THEY FOUND **ME** INSTEAD.

DO YOU KNOW WHAT IT'S *LIKE?* TO HAVE A CAST OF *THOUSANDS* CHURNING IN YOUR GUTS?

SPEAKING *THROUGH* YOU? SCREAMING TO BE *FED?*

GUUH!

BUT THEN AGAIN, I GET TO HAVE MY OWN RELIGION. BECAUSE THE MOUTHS *PROPHESY* SOMETIMES.

AND EVERY-ONE LINES UP TO DROP THEIR PANTS FOR A FUCKING *MESSIAH.*

SHE WILL SPEAK YOUR *NAME,* CONSTANTINE. SPEAK IT THREE TIMES--AND YOU WILL *FALL* THREE TIMES.

INCEST, JOHN! ASK HER WHO HER FATHER WAS. HEH HEH HEH!

AND SPEAK OF THE *DEVIL*--

YOU'VE GOT THEM ALL *EXCITED.* THEY THINK THEY'RE GOING TO BE *EATING* YOU TONIGHT.

BUT THAT'D BE TOO QUICK. TOO *EASY.*

WHATEVER I DO TO YOU-- *TRUST* ME ON THIS--

--IT'S GOING TO LAST *FOREVER.*

BROTHERS AND SISTERS!

LISTEN TO ME, PLEASE!

YOU'RE DISTURBED AND YOU'RE AFRAID. WELL, THAT'S *NATURAL*. SO AM I.

BEING AFRAID ISN'T A *SIN*. IT DOESN'T MEAN YOU'RE NOT AMONG THE RIGHTEOUS.

THAT THING THAT THE SAVIOR CALLS *CONSTANTINE*--

IT WALKED AMONG YOU--SPOKE TO YOU--PERHAPS EVEN *TOUCHED* YOU.

AND NOW WE KNOW IT WAS A LIMB OF THE *BEAST*, OUT FISHING FOR OUR SOULS.

WHAT COULD BE MORE FRIGHTENING THAN *THAT?*

THE SAVIOR HAS FOUGHT IT *BEFORE.*

THINK OF *THAT.* THINK OF WHAT THAT MEANS.

AN EVIL SO POWERFUL--

--IT CONTENDED AGAINST THE *SAVIOR* AND IT LIVED TO WALK AWAY.

AND SO I *KNEEL*--IN FRONT OF ALL OF YOU, IN FRONT OF GOD AND MAN, I KNEEL.

I *BLESS* THE FEET THAT TROD HIM DOWN. I KISS THE HAND THAT *SMOTE.*

FOR HOW ELSE WILL THE SOULS THAT FELL TO THE BEAST FIND THEIR WAY *HOME* AGAIN--

--SAVE BY WALKING THE ROAD OF ITS FOUL *BLOOD?*

AMEN!

AMEN!

AMEN!

AMEN!

AMEN!

AMEN!

AMEN!

108

WELL, WHAT ARE WE GOING TO DO WITH HIM?

WHAT WOULD REALLY, REALLY *HURT*?

YOU COULD PUT OUT HIS EYES.

AND CUT OFF HIS LIMBS.

SEPARATE HIM FROM THE WORLD.

THAT'S JUST *CRUDE*.

HAVE HIM RAPED BY SYPHILITIC INCUBI. TURN HIM INTO A DISEASE FARM.

NEXT.

GIVE HIM TO US.

BEFORE HE *TRICKS YOU* AND DESTROYS YOU, AS HE DOES EVERYONE.

NO. I'VE GOT A *BETTER* IDEA.

LOOK... YOU'VE GOT TO **HELP** ME.

YOUR SAVIOR IS A FUCKING **PSYCHOPATH.**

AND I MUST'VE **PISSED** HIM **OFF** IN A PREVIOUS LIFE, BECAUSE--

WHUMP

KKHHHHH!

HAVEN'T YOU **LEARNED** YET, DEMON? I'VE JUST GOT THE ONE ANSWER FOR YOU.

SHIT, DON'T EVEN **TALK** TO HIM, DARREN! HE'LL TEMPT YOU!

I'M ARMORED IN **RIGHTEOUSNESS.**

THE LORD IS MY SHEPHERD AND THE **SAVIOR** IS MY SHIELD.

LOOK, I'M **NOT** THE BEAST.

THINK ABOUT THIS RATIONALLY. **LOOK** AT ME-- JUST LOOK AT ME.

AAAAH!

CHRIST!

I--

--I THINK I'VE LOST MY **FAITH**.

TCHOKK

OKAY. I ADMIT I DIDN'T QUITE GET THAT.

THERE WAS A BOY NAMED HUGHIE.

HE WAS WELSH AND HE HAD A SILLY ACCENT.

HE WAS THE ONE I BROUGHT IN BEFORE YOU, AND HE--

--HE DISAPPEARED. A LOT OF PEOPLE DO AROUND HERE.

WHUMP WHUMP

JESUS! IS THERE ANOTHER WAY OUT?

THAT DOOR ISN'T GOING TO--

OH.

THIS-- THIS ISN'T THE RIGHT *WAY*.

WELL, WE CAN'T GO *BACK*. WE'LL HAVE TO TRY THE LOWER LEVELS.

BUT I DON'T *KNOW* THEM!

THIS WAY!

TAKE IT *SLOW*, WE'LL GET THEM.

THAT *BITCH* IS GOING TO *BURN* FOR THIS!

YOU ARE GHANT?

YEAH. YES, I'M GHANT.

YOU'RE THE *FIRST*. MAKE YOURSELF AT *HOME*.

YOU COULD NOT EVEN *IMAGINE* MY HOME.

WHERE IS HE?

I'M SORRY! I'M SORRY!

I COULDN'T *HELP* IT, IT JUST--

IT'S OKAY. AT LEAST SOME OF THE BASTARDS WILL HAVE BURST *EAR-DRUMS.*

FUCK!

WHAT THE--?

DON'T MOVE!

I MEAN, THROW YOURSELF *FLAT!*

HOW CAN YOU HAVE *QUICKSAND* IN A BASEMENT? IT'S FUCKING *RIDICULOUS!*

LET GO.

LET GO OF MY *HAND* OR YOU'LL BE--

AAAAAAA!

YOU SEE, THIS ISN'T GOING TO BE A *REGULAR* AUCTION.

AS FAR AS THAT GOES, THERE'S ONLY ONE BID I'LL *LISTEN* TO.

I WANT THESE SPIRITS *BURNED* OUT OF MY FLESH!

I WANT TO BE *ALONE* IN MY OWN FUCKING HEAD!

ANY OF US COULD DO THAT. MOST OF US WITH A *GESTURE.*

SO HOW WILL YOU DISTINGUISH *BETWEEN* US?

EASY. YOU TELL ME HOW YOU'RE GOING TO *DO* HIM.

HOW YOU'RE GOING TO *HURT* HIM.

POINTS WILL BE AWARDED FOR TECHNICAL *MERIT* AND ARTISTIC *EFFECT.*

FORGET *ME,* YOU BASTARD?

YOU'LL *NEVER* FORGET ME NOW...

129

"...NOT AS LONG AS YOU FUCKING *LIVE*."

YOU'RE OUT OF YOUR BLOODY *MIND*.

YOU *KNOW* THAT?

IT *WORKS*, CONSTANTINE. THERE'S POWER IN THIS.

REAL POWER.

THERE'S POWER IN THE NATIONAL *GRID* TOO, BUT YOU WOULDN'T STICK YOUR FINGER IN THE FUCKING *WALL SOCKET*.

COCCYX. CARPALS. COSTALS. CRANIUM.

MALLEUS. INCUS. CALCANEUS.

THE TOE BONE'S CONNECTED-- CONNECTED--

HHHHHHHH!

YESSSS!

JESUS!

I SEE THE *FUTURE*, JOHN. I SEE YOU BOUGHT AND *SOLD* AT MY WHIM.

I'M GONNA HAVE *SUCH* A FUCKING GOOD TIME.

"GIVE HIM TO *ME*..."

...I'LL GROW A MILLION CONSTANTINES, AND MOVE HIS *SOUL* FROM ONE TO THE NEXT.

KILLING *EACH* IN SOME UNIQUE AND DIVERTING WAY.

TORMENTS OF THE *FLESH*, ONLY. I'LL CORRUPT HIM, AND DRIVE HIM *MAD*.

MAKE HIM RAPE AND MURDER THOSE HE *LOVES*, SO HE SEES CLEARLY EVERYTHING HE'S DONE.

THE EXTREMES OF PAIN ARE ONLY REACHED THROUGH PLEASURE.

WE WOULD RAISE HIM TO THE GREATEST *HEIGHT*, THAT HIS FALL WOULD BE THE MORE *AGONIZING.*

WHAT?

DID YOU *COME* HERE TO SEE CONSTANTINE BLEED OR PIMP YOUR SISTER?

YOU SPEAK WITH *SCANT* RESPECT.

GOOD. BECAUSE SCANT RESPECT IS WHAT I'M *FEELING.*

WHOEVER GAVE YOU WHIP-LICKING *PERVERTS* A VOICE IN HELL'S AFFAIRS HAS GOT A LOT TO--

--TO--

....

131

MAJESTY I-- I NEVER MEANT TO QUESTION--

MY JUDGMENT?

BUT AGONY AND ECSTASY DATE BACK TO LUCIFER'S TIME. THEY'RE NOT MINE.

BESIDES, YOUR HONESTY IS REFRESHING.

YOU SHOULDN'T BE ASHAMED OF IT.

FIRST AMONG THE FALLEN, I--I'M HONORED. DEEPLY HONORED THAT YOU'VE COME.

AND YET YOU DIDN'T INVITE ME. WHY WAS THAT?

BECAUSE YOU WERE AFRAID OF ME. IT'S UNDERSTANDABLE.

BUT NOW THAT I'M HERE, I IMAGINE YOU FEEL AN URGENT--ALMOST DESPERATE NEED--

--TO MAKE AMENDS FOR MY HURT FEELINGS.

THE AUCTION'S *CANCELLED.*

YOU CAN ALL FUCK *OFF.*

I GIVE THESE TWO SOULS INTO YOUR *KEEPING,* FIRST AMONG THE FALLEN.

I HOPE THIS OFFERING FINDS *FAVOR* IN YOUR EYES.

MY *EYES?* WHAT ABOUT MY *EARS?*

YOUR--?

THE *GAG,* YOU CRETIN. TAKE OFF THE *GAG.*

IT'S THE *GLOATING* THAT MAKES THIS WORTHWHILE, NOT THE *EVISCERATION.*

SO. IT'S BEEN A *WHILE*, HASN'T IT?

YEAH. AGES.

AGES AND AGES AND AGES.

AND NOW YOU'VE *GOT* ME. AT LAST.

LET'S GET IT OVER WITH *QUICKLY*, EH? LET'S JUST DO IT WITHOUT *TALKING* ABOUT IT.

NOW. RIGHT NOW.

HAVE YOU DONE SOMETHING TO HIS *MIND*?

NO! HIS *MEMORY'S* FUCKED, THAT'S ALL.

HE DOESN'T KNOW WHO HE *IS* ANYMORE.

THAT'S A *PITY*. IT CERTAINLY TAKES AWAY SOME OF THE--

I'M *CONSTANTINE!*

WHAT?

I'M JOHN CONSTANTINE, HONEST TO *GOD!*

WHAT ARE YOU *WAITING* FOR? YOU KNOW HOW *FUCKING* *DANGEROUS* I AM.

YOU KNOW WHAT ALWAYS *HAPPENS* WHEN I'M IN A CORNER. JUST *DO* IT!

I'M THE-- THE SCOURGE OF *HELL!* I'M THE BASTARD WHO *SCREWS* THE DEVIL!

I'M--

SHIT. OH, SHIT.

I FORGET THE WORDS, MISTER GHANT.

I'M SORRY. I'M SORRY.

LET ME TRY *AGAIN.* PLEASE! I *PROMISE* I'LL GET IT RIGHT.

SO YOU *COACHED* HIM IN THIS ROLE.

TELL ME--DID YOU FIND HIM, OR *MAKE* HIM?

WHAAAAT?

BUT IT'S A *LIE!*

IT'S A FUCKING *OBVIOUS* LIE.

YES. *NOW* IT IS.

"HE'S LOST HIS *MEMORY.*" SO HE CAN'T BE *QUESTIONED.*

SO HE ONLY HAS TO *SOUND* LIKE CONSTANTINE FOR A FEW FLEETING SECONDS.

NO! NO! *NO!*

I--I CAN *PROVE* THAT HE'S THE REAL CONSTANTINE.

LOOK AT HIS *ARSE!* HE'S GOT A *TREE* TATTOOED ON HIS ARSE.

HIS *ARSE?*

YOU WANT ME TO SNIFF AT HIS *RECTUM?* LIKE A *DOG?*

137

YOU. AND YOU. YOU'RE WORKING FOR *ME*, NOW.

PICK HIM UP AND *FOLLOW* ME.

NO! NO, THIS IS FUCKING *INSANE!*

YOU'RE NOT GOING TO LET HIM GET *AWAY* WITH THIS. YOU CAN'T--

BRING THEM.

BRING THEM UNTO GOLGOTHA!

AW NO. YOU'VE GOT TO BE BLOODY JOKING.

PLEASE! MARGARET, PLEASE DON'T *DO* THIS!

IT'S ME. IT'S SUZIE. I'M YOUR *FRIEND* IN CHRIST.

PTOO

IF EITHER OF YOU WANTS TO *PRAY*, AND KISS THE BOOK--

THE LORD MIGHT HAVE *MERCY* ON YOUR SOULS, AFTER THE WINNOWING OF YOUR *FLESH*.

FUCK OFF OUT OF IT, YOU GOD-BOTHERING PIECE OF *SHIT*.

THEN BURN--

--AND BE *DAMNED* TO YOU BOTH.

OH SWEET *JESUS!* I DON'T WANT TO *BURN.*

YOU DON'T-- *;COF!;--HAVE* TO. JUST BREATHE IN THE SMOKE.

THAT'LL KILL YOU *FIRST.*

WHAT DO YOU THINK OF MY OFFER *NOW,* JOHN?

BE HONEST. AREN'T YOU *TEMPTED?*

I TOLD YOU IN *HELL!* I FUCKING *TOLD* YOU--

I KNOW.

BUT I THOUGHT YOU MIGHT WANT TO CHANGE YOUR *MIND.*

ONE DAY. ONE DAY IN MY *SERVICE.*

AND IN RETURN YOU GET TO *LIVE.* WITH ALL YOUR *MEMORIES* BACK WHERE THEY BELONG.

ARRHHH!

F-FUCK! OH *FUCK!*

GUUH! ALL RIGHT, I'LL DO IT.

BUT WHAT ABOUT *SUZIE?* I'M NOT LEAVING HER TO *DIE* HERE.

MMMMM...

OKAY.

TSCH-
RAKKK

OH JESUS!

OH NO NO NOOOOO!

IT'S THE **SMALL** THINGS I APPRECIATE THE MOST.

I MEAN, A FUCKING **ALLOTMENT.** WHAT WOULD THE BIG GREEN BLOKE HAVE TO SAY ABOUT **THAT** ONE?

I'M FALLING AND FLOUNDERING AND **SINKING** IN BITTER BLACK BILE.

THERE'S NO **DAYLIGHT!** THERE'S NO FUCKING DAYLIGHT!

I TAKE A **WALK** EVERY NOW AND THEN UP TO WATERLOO BRIDGE. WATCH THE RIVER GO BY AND THINK, YEAH, IT'S **FINISHED** NOW.

IT JUST GIVES ME AN ENORMOUS SENSE OF **RELIEF**--THAT I'M THROUGH WITH IT. ALL THE **BULLSHIT.**

NO! GET **ME** OUT OF THIS!

FOR THE LOVE OF **CHRIST**--

AND DOWN THE **PUB** THE OTHER NIGHT CHAS STARTED IN WITH SOME STORY ABOUT WHEN WE WERE **BAD** LADS.

I SWEAR IT FELT LIKE SOMEONE **ELSE.** SOMEONE I DIDN'T EVEN RECOGNIZE.

SO I WAKE UP THIS MORNING FEELING REALLY *BAD*.

LIKE SOMONE *FUCKED* ME THROUGH A HOLE IN THE BACK OF MY SKULL.

CAN'T TAKE MY *ALE* ANYMORE.

AND THE HELL OF IT IS, I DON'T *WANT* TO.

DON'T WANT TO LOOK IN THE *MIRROR* ANYMORE, EITHER.

SHAVE *ELECTRIC*, BY FEEL, SO I DON'T HAVE TO LOOK AT MY DAD'S *FACE* STARING BACK AT ME.

OVERSLEPT AGAIN. *EL DORADO* OPENS AT ELEVEN.

BUT I'M IN NO HURRY. *NEWLAND* WILL WANT A LITTLE WORD, AND I'M NOT *UP* FOR THAT JUST YET.

ANYWAY, I NEVER WATCHED THE *CLOCK* IN MY LIFE.

I'M NOT GONNA START *NOW*.

WELL, YOU TOOK YOUR OWN SWEET *TIME*, MISTER.

NOW WHAT KIND OF TALK IS THAT, EH, KIT?

I'M *MARRIED* TO YOU, JOHN CONSTANTINE.

YOU CAN SAVE THE RAKISH CHARM FOR SUCH AS MIGHT *SWALLOW* IT.

CROSS MY HEART--YOU'LL GET YOUR PRESENT *TONIGHT.* IT'S ALL SET UP.

AYE, WELL, I'LL *WAIT.*

I WAITED LONG ENOUGH FOR *YOU,* GOD KNOWS.

OH, AND YOU'VE TO DROP *ADAM* AT MRS. DASK'S. I KNOW HE DOESN'T *LIKE* HER, BUT I'VE GOT TO GO INTO THE GARAGE TODAY.

WE'VE THE *V.A.T.* IN, GOD HELP US.

DOES UNCLE CHAS *WORK* FOR MUMMY?

NO, THEY JUST WORK AT THE SAME *PLACE.*

WELL, DOES MUMMY WORK FOR UNCLE *CHAS,* THEN?

DON'T BE *DAFT!*

KIT'S PICKING HIM UP, MRS. D.

ALL RIGHT, JOHN. WHAT WILL WE DO *TODAY,* ADAM?

SOME *PAINTING?*

I'VE BEEN PUTTING THIS OFF FOR TWO BLOODY *WEEKS.*

BUT IT'S ALWAYS *BETTER* TO GO TO MONTY NEWLAND BEFORE *HE* COMES TO YOU.

EL DORADO CASINO

BIG PRIZES! GUARANTEED 98% PAY OUT DAILY

FRANKLY, JOHN, I'M NOT *HAPPY*--

I'M NOT HAPPY AT *ALL.*

THERE'S A *LOT OF* PEOPLE WANT TO HUSTLE AT MY TABLES. SO I SET A COMPETITIVE *RATE.*

IT'S FIVE TON A WEEK, AND YOU OWE ME A FUCKING *MONTH'S WORTH* OF BACK RENT.

I *KNOW* THAT, MONTY. I'M NOT TRYING TO--

I DO *NOT* GIVE CREDIT. I DO *NOT* MAKE EXCEPTIONS.

I WANT THAT EFFING *MONEY* WHEN I OPEN UP TOMORROW.

SO I GO *DOWNSTAIRS.* GET INTO A GAME BY PULLING THE "OH, ARE THESE THINGS *PLAYING* CARDS?" ROUTINE.

FUCK, THOUGH. TWO *GRAND* BY TOMORROW MORNING. THAT'S A TALL ORDER.

AND I DUNNO WHAT IT IS, BUT MY *LUCK'S* FLATTER THAN MY GRANNY'S TITS LATELY.

IF IT WAS RAINING *SOUP,* I'D HAVE A FORK. RIGHT THROUGH MY *EYEBALL.*

I TURN IN AFTER A FEW HOURS, ONLY FIFTY QUID *UP.*

THOUGHT I MIGHT DROP IN ON KIT, BUT WHEN I'M PASSING THE *CHILDMINDER'S* HOUSE I SEE THE AMBULANCE AND THE PADDY WAGON.

WHAT'S *HAPPENED?*

WHAT THE FUCK HAS *HAPPENED?!*

DADDY!

ADAM! OH THANK CHRIST!

ALL RIGHT, MARK. I THINK WE'VE *LOCATED* THAT LAST PARENT.

SO YOU *KNEW* IRENE DASK, DID YOU, MISTER--?

JOHN CONSTANTINE. SHE LOOKS AFTER MY *SON* ON ODD DAYS.

WHAT DO YOU MEAN BY "*KNEW*"?

WE'RE ASSUMING SHE HAD AN *ACCIDENT.* BUT IT'S HARD TO CREDIT.

MRS. DASK WAS A DIABETIC, ON AN *INSULIN* REGIME.

ONLY TODAY IT WAS A *DRAIN* CLEANER REGIME.

HELL OF A WAY TO *GO.*

THEY SAID THE KIDS HAD BEEN SITTING WITH THE *BODY* FOR AN HOUR AND A HALF.

I SUPPOSE ADAM'S TOO YOUNG TO *UNDERSTAND* DEATH. AND KIDS ARE *TOUGH*--THEY BOUNCE BACK FROM ANYTHING. STILL...

AND THESE ARE THE *WILD* THINGS, DANCING.

THE WILD *RUMPUS!*

THE WILD RUMPUS.

BLOW IT OUT? OUR *ANNIVERSARY* DINNER?

WELL, JUST PUT IT *BACK* A DAY OR SO.

I DON'T THINK WE SHOULD LEAVE HIM *ALONE* TONIGHT.

JOHN, TRISH WILL *CALL* US IF THERE'S ANY PROBLEM. WE'RE NOT GOING TO THE END OF THE BLOODY WORLD.

AND HE NEVER EVEN *LIKED* THE WOMAN. PERHAPS IT'S ALL FOR THE *BEST.*

"ALL FOR THE BEST"?

YEAH.

WELL, KIT GREW UP IN BELFAST. I SUPPOSE THAT MAKES YOU A BIT HARD, LIKE.

AND SHACKING UP WITH YOU, AND ALL. NOT FOR THE FAINT-HEARTED, IS IT?

REMEMBER WHEN WE BLAGGED THAT CRUCIFIX THAT WOULDN'T STOP BLEEDING? DID YOU EVER TELL HER ABOUT THAT?

PROBABLY NOT. LISTEN, IS YOUR TRISH STILL OKAY FOR SITTING TONIGHT?

DO WHAT? YOU KNOW HOW SHE IS WITH KIDS. SHE'S NOT GONNA MISS A CHANCE TO--

CONSTANTINE!

MONTY.

DID YOU THINK I WAS JOKING?

NO. RIGHT. TOMORROW WE SAID, YEAH? ON THE DOT OF ELEVEN.

YOU SHOULD NOT BE DOWN HERE ON THE PISS.

YOU SHOULD BE COUNTING UP YOUR PENNIES AND MAKING SURE YOU GET THE RIGHT FUCKING ANSWER.

WHAT'S GOING **ON**?

JOHN? ARE YOU OKAY?

YOU'VE GOT TO GET **OUT** OF HERE, MATE. YOU OWED THAT BASTARD **MONEY**!

WHY THE FUCK IS THIS **HAPPENING**? AND WHY **NOW**?

SOMEONE WITH AN OLD **GRUDGE**, LETTING ME KNOW I'M VULNERABLE?

BUT IN THAT CASE WHY KILL **NEWLAND**? YOU'D EXPECT THEM TO GO FOR--

OH CHRIST!

OH JESUS SUFFERING **CHRIST**!

CALL THEM, JOHN.

THERE'S A **PHONE** AT THE CORNER. CALL THEM!

COME ON, COME **ON**!

PICK **UP**!

HELLO? OH *HI*, JOHN! WHAT? I CAN'T *HEAR* YOU.

NO. NO, WE'RE ALL FINE. KIT'S JUST GONE ON TO THE *RESTAURANT*.

AND I'M ABOUT TO PUT HIS *NIBS* TO BED.

I'M NOT *READY* FOR BED YET.

RIGHT. LOOK, DON'T OPEN THE DOOR TO ANYONE, TRISH.

AND CALL US ON KIT'S *MOBILE* IF--WELL, IF ANYTHING HAPPENS. *ANYTHING*, OKAY?

ALL CLEAR, RIGHT? NOTHING TO *WORRY* ABOUT?

NOT MUCH, NO. JUST A BODY COUNT OF *THREE* ON MY SODDING ANNIVERSARY.

NEVER *MIND*.

OKAY, YOU LITTLE *MONSTER*.

TIME'S UP.

CLICK

SO THE GYPSY VIOLINIST ISN'T **COMING**, THEN?

DAVID **BLUNKETT** PUT HIM ON A BOAT HOME.

I'LL PLAY YOU SOMETHING ON THE **SPOONS**.

HERE'S TO **US**, JOHN. AND TO POSTERITY.

OH, YES. I'M IN FOR THE LONG **HAUL**, MISTER.

POSTERITY?

I CAN'T QUITE **DO** IT TONIGHT. THE SMALL TALK. THE YOUR-TURN-MY-TURN STUFF.

KIT RATTLES ON, BUT MY MIND'S STUCK IN A **GROOVE**.

NOTHING FOR FIVE YEARS. AND THEN INSIDE OF A DAY--

--A SINGLE **DAY** OF MY LIFE--

IT'S LIKE I'VE BEEN **ASLEEP**. I'VE LET THINGS CREEP UP ON ME. **OVER** ME.

"PARANOIA, JOHN," RICK THE VIC SAID TO ME ONCE. "PARANOIA'S YOUR BEST BLOODY **FRIEND**."

YOU JUST TURNED YOUR *PHONE* OFF.

SO? DON'T WE *DESERVE* OUR PRIVACY TONIGHT?

WHAT'S HAPPENING AT THE *HOUSE?*

SURE, IT'S A RITE OF *PASSAGE,* JOHN. I HADN'T EXPECTED IT SO SOON.

BUT OUR LITTLE BOY IS TURNING INTO A *MAN.*

HEY. ANOTHER *BOTTLE* HERE.

CAN'T YOU SEE WE'RE *CELEBRATING?*

DON'T KNOW WHY I'M *RUNNING.* DON'T KNOW WHY I'M SO *SCARED.*

THERE ARE *HOLES.* HOLES IN MY LIFE.

ALL OF A SUDDEN *NOTHING* MAKES ANY SENSE.

TRISH?

WHERE'S *ADAM?* IS EVERYTHING OKAY?

TRISH?

163

HELLO, DADDY.

YOU'RE BACK EARLY.

WHAT *HAPPENED?*

ADAM, WHAT IN *GOD'S* NAME HAPPENED TO HER?

YOU SHOULDN'T TALK ABOUT GOD, DADDY. MAM DOESN'T LIKE THAT.

I *TOLD* HER I WASN'T READY TO GO TO BED YET.

BUT SHE DIDN'T *LISTEN.*

WHAT DID YOU *DO?*

I MADE HER *SEE* STUFF.

ALL THE STUFF SHE'S *SCARED* OF.

IT WAS *HARDER* WHEN I GOT THAT MAN TO USE THE GUN.

BUT MRS. DASK WAS *EASY* BECAUSE SHE WAS *OLD.*

164

ADAM I DON'T UNDER-STAND *ANY* OF THIS.

BUT WHAT YOU'VE DONE--OH, *CHRIST*, I CAN'T LET YOU--
...

VERY GOOD, ADAM. IS IT *EASIER* NOW?

MUCH EASIER, MAM. SHALL I HOLD HIM STILL?

HOLD HIM *VERY* STILL, LOVE.

YOU PROMISED ME A FULL *DAY* OF YOUR LIFE, JOHN.

AND THE SUN HAS BARELY *RISEN* ON THAT DAY...

CLICK

IT'S ALL *DOWNHILL* FROM HERE.

SAUL, THIS IS *INCREDIBLE*.

HIS ROOTS GO *DEEP* INTO THE WORLD-- LIKE MINE.

YEAH, BUT STILL. I'VE ONLY BEEN *GONE* TWO WEEKS!

"HYBRID VIGOR." I'VE GOT MY *OWN* MAGIC, DAD.

AND MY OWN SECRETS. I'VE TAKEN OVER THE *GREEN-HOUSE*, IF THAT'S OKAY.

ABBY *CABLE*?

WHAT THE FUCK WAS ABBY CABLE DOING IN *SCOTLAND*?

THIS IS SAUL'S END-OF-YEAR *PROJECT*. HE'S HOPING FOR A DISTINCTION.

THAT'S GREAT.

HE'S ALREADY HAD A *JOB* OFFER FROM THE AGRICULTURAL COLLEGE.

"LANDSCAPE GARDENING"? I JUST *LAUGHED*.

I SAID I WANT TO WORK WITH THE *WILD* EARTH. THE DARK AND SECRET SOIL.

ABSOLUTELY!

CAN'T GET THAT OUT OF MY MIND.

WHERE WAS SHE GOING?

WHO WAS SHE LOOKING FOR?

JOHN, IS THERE SOMETHING THE *MATTER*?

YOU'VE HARDLY SAID A *WORD* SINCE YOU GOT BACK.

WHAT? NO. I WAS JUST THINKING ABOUT THESE *DISAPPEARANCES*.

WONDERING IF THERE WAS ANYTHING *TO* THEM. A PATTERN, OR--

OH, IT WAS ON THE *RADIO* JUST NOW. SOME HOMELESS BLOKE IN ARBROATH *KILLED* HIMSELF AND LEFT A CONFESSION.

THEY'RE TRAWLING LUNAN BAY FOR THE BODIES.

ALL'S WELL THAT *ENDS* WELL, THEN.

TRY THE *WINE*, JOHN. SAUL PRESSED IT HIMSELF.

ALL'S WELL THAT *ENDS* WELL.

AND EVERYTHING'S FOR THE *BEST*, AFTER ALL.

LOVELY. REALLY *SMOOTH*.

AND COUNT YOUR *BLESSINGS*.

BUT THE FEELING OF *DREAD* GROWS IN ME AS THE DAYS GO BY.

THUNDER RUMBLES ON THE *HORIZON*, ENDLESSLY THREATENING, BUT THE STORM NEVER

CORN SHOULD BE *UP* BY NOW. BUT IT'S BEEN A BAD SPRING *EVERYWHERE*, JOHN.

EXCEPT IN YOUR GARDEN. THAT WEE BIT *LAD* OF YOURS, HE'S A MARVEL.

ZED DOESN'T *LIKE* ME DOING MAGIC. BUT THERE'S NO HARM IN A BIT OF *MEDITATION*.

FINDING THE *CENTER*. BECAUSE CHRIST KNOWS, I'M FUCKING *LOST* AT THE MOMENT.

MY MIND SLIPS OUT OF *ONE* GROOVE INTO ANOTHER. BEEN A WHILE, BUT YOU NEVER LOSE THE *KNACK*.

EVERYTHING IN THE ROOM BECOMES *LUMINOUS* WITH ITS OWN INNER LIGHT.

AND THEN THE ROOM GOES *AWAY*.

DROPS LIKE A *STONE* INTO A WELL. OR MAYBE IT'S *ME* THAT'S DROPPING.

WIND WHISTLING PAST ME. REALITY *SHRINKING* TO A BALL OF LIGHT LIKE THE EYE OF GOD.

AND AS THE EYE *CLOSES*--

--I SNAP *OUT* OF IT. MY *FEAR* BREAKS THE TRANCE.

OR MAYBE IT WAS THE *SOUND* FROM OUTSIDE. THE CAR HORN BLARING LIKE A SOUL IN *TORMENT*.

DISTANT RUMBLE OF THUNDER LIKE THE DEVIL MOVING THE FURNITURE AROUND.

SOMETHING'S *WRONG*.

SOMETHING'S SO *VERY* WRONG.

CRASH

JOHN, STAY OUT OF THIS! IT DOESN'T *CONCERN* YOU!

SOD *THAT!*

OH CHRIST ON A *BIKE!* GEMMA!

SAU-- SAUL--

NO, IT'S *ME*-- JOHN.

HE'S TORTURING--THE *GREEN*--

UNCLE JOHN! YOU'VE GOT TO--

THE *SMELL* HITS ME FIRST.

LIKE A FRIDGE FULL OF SPOILED *MEAT.*

LIKE A BODY BAG, RIPENED IN THE *SUN* UNTIL IT SPLITS.

THEN THE *SOUNDS.*

SIGHING OF *LEAVES* IN A WIND I CAN'T FEEL.

WHISPERING *PLEAS* FROM DRY, CRACKED THROATS.

THE THUNDER *WASN'T* ON THE HORIZON.

THE STORM *WASN'T GATHERING.* NOT AT ALL.

THE SIGN SAYS KEEP *OUT,* DAD.

YOU REALLY *NEED* TO RESPECT MY SPACE.

WHY, SAUL? WHY DID YOU *DO* THIS?

OH, YOU KNOW. LIFE IS *MOSTLY* A WASTE OF TIME.

BUT IT MAKES SOM INTERESTING *NOISES* WHEN YOU SQUEEZE IT

SOME-THING'S TAKEN YOU *OVER.* POSSESSED YOU--

NO, DAD. I PRETTY MUCH *CAME* THIS WAY.

IT'S JUST YOUR REFRESHING *CYNICISM,* TWEAKED UP A NOTCH OR TWO.

THEN I'M *SORRY,* SON.

I'M REALLY, REALLY SORRY.

THWUK

WELL THAT'S-- THAT'S *HURTFUL,* DAD.

NOT *SURPRISING,* I SUPPOSE. BUT STILL NOT NICE.

THANK YOU FOR COMING **IN**, MR. AND MRS. CONSTANTINE.

WE HAVE **SEVERAL** CONCERNS, AND MOST OF THEM YOU ALREADY KNOW.

BUT FRANKLY, THE STICKING POINT FOR US IS THE **HOCKEY** INCIDENT.

THE OTHER GIRL IS STILL IN HOSPITAL. SHE MAY **NEVER** FULLY RECOVER.

THAT WAS AN **ACCIDENT**.

SO I'M RECOMMENDING **EXPULSION** RATHER THAN SUSPENSION. I'M VERY SORRY.

DID YOU HAVE ANY **QUESTIONS**?

YEAH, I'VE GOT TWO. OFF THE TOP OF MY **HEAD**, LIKE.

YES, WELL. SO MARIA **SAYS**.

BUT THERE HAVE BEEN SO **MANY** VIOLENT INCIDENTS. THERE **IS** A PATTERN.

WHERE WERE YOU **BORN**?

AND WHAT WAS YOUR **MOTHER'S** NAME?

I'M SORRY, MISTER CONSTANTINE, I DON'T--

ARE YOU MARRIED? GOT ANY KIDS? WHERE DO YOU LIVE?

I DON'T REALLY SEE--

WHAT'S IN THE DESK DRAWER?

I DON'T THINK THIS *INTERVIEW* IS SERVING ANY--

WHAT'S IN THE FUCKING *DESK* DRAWER?

IT'S *YOURS*, ISN'T IT? YOUR STUFF? FUCKING *ANSWER* ME!

JOHN, STOP! YOU'RE *EMBARRASSING* ME!

M-MY DIARY. SOME *PENS.*

A *CIRCULAR* FROM THE EDUCATION AUTHORITY--

EMPTY. *GOT* YOU, YOU BASTARDS.

WE LEAVE THE HEAD *BLUSTERING* ABOUT LUNACY, LAWSUITS AND LIKE FATHER LIKE DAUGHTER.

ANGIE WON'T LOOK AT ME, AND I DON'T *BLAME* HER.

AND I DON'T *CARE*.

BACK AT THE CAFÉ I GO THROUGH THE CUT-UP *PAPERS* WE WRAP THE CHIPS IN.

IS THIS *ME?* LETTING THE WORLD SLIDE *PAST* ME IN GREASE-SLICKED NEWSPRINT?

IN A *TRANCE* FOR FOURTEEN YEARS?

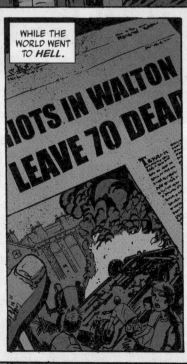

WHILE THE WORLD WENT TO *HELL.*

RIOTS IN WALTON LEAVE 70 DEAD

OR HELL CAME UP AND *MET* IT HALFWAY.

HI, DAD.

THERE'S A *SLEEP-OVER* AT SHONA'S TONIGHT.

CAN I GO?

MARIA? MARIA **CONSTANTINE?**

UH... YE-EAH. DAD, ARE YOU **DRUNK** AGAIN?

I-- HAVE I BEEN THERE WHEN YOU **NEEDED** ME?

DO YOU NEED ME **NOW?** IS SOMETHING-- IS THERE ANY-THING--?

COME ON, MARIA. LET'S **GO.**

ALL I NEED FROM YOU IS A **YES,** DAD.

AND MAYBE A **FIVER** FOR A GAME RENTAL.

NO, WAIT! I FEEL LIKE I'VE **MISSED** SOMETHING.

EVERYTHING. I WANT TO **KNOW** YOU.

JESUS! YOU'RE COMING ON LIKE A **FUCKED-UP** OLD **PEDO,** DAD. WE **BURN** PEOPLE LIKE THAT.

WELL, MY DIARY'S UNDER THE LOOSE **FLOORBOARD,** YEAH?

YOU CAN GO AND HAVE A BIT OF A WANK OVER **THAT.**

SHE DOESN'T LOOK *BACK*.

FOURTEEN YEARS *OLD*. SHE'S GOT THINGS TO DO. PLACES TO BE.

THE STUFF OF MY NIGHTMARES, THROWN LIKE *DUST SHEETS* OVER THE WORLD.

DISGUISING *EVERYTHING*.

AND I'VE CAUGHT REALITY OUT IN A BARE-FACED *LIE*. BUT I STILL CAN'T WAKE UP.

AND I CAN'T SHAKE THE FEELING THAT I'M IN A *FIGHT* I'VE ALREADY LOST.

OH SHIT! I GOT *BLOOD* ON MY TIGHTS!

HEY, IT'S *MY* TURN. YOU ALREADY HAD A GO!

LOOK IN HIS *EYES*.

YOU CAN SEE HE'S *FEELING* IT.

EYES, *PLURAL*?

I THINK YOU LOST *COUNT*, SHONA.

WHOA! FUUUUUUUCK!

YOU'LL *REMEMBER* SAUL, AND ADAM.

YOU'LL REMEMBER *EVERYTHING*, NOW. THAT'S MY PARTING GIFT TO YOU.

THAT'S THREE FOR *THREE*, JOHN.

THEY ALL KICKED THE SHIT OUT OF YOU. I'M SO PROUD.

YOU'RE NOT EVEN *HUMAN*, ARE YOU?

GOD, NO!

DID YOU *REALLY* GO TO ALL THIS TROUBLE JUST TO GET YOUR LEG OVER ME?

TO *BREED* WITH YOU, JOHN.

TO BEAR *CHILDREN* WITH YOUR UNIQUE--QUALITIES. AND THEN TO HAVE YOU *RAISE* THEM FOR ME.

SO THEY'VE GOT YOUR *NUMBER*, AS WELL AS YOUR GENES. SO THEY *KNOW* YOU.

THE WAY YOU *THINK*. THE WAY YOU *FIGHT*. THE THINGS YOU *LOVE* AND THE THINGS YOU *FEAR*.

I DON'T **SEE** IT, MOTHER. WE'VE TAKEN EVERYTHING WE **NEED** FROM HIM.

WHY NOT PUT HIM OUT OF HIS **MISERY?**

BECAUSE WE **LIKE** HIS MISERY, SAUL. IT'S PART OF THE **POINT.**

YOU BURY ME IN A **DREAM.** STEAL HALF MY **LIFE.**

THIS WON'T BE **OVER** UNTIL YOU KILL ME, LOVE. YOU MUST **KNOW** THAT.

YOU'RE **MISTAKEN,** JOHN.

I TOOK EXACTLY **ONE** DAY. AS WE AGREED.

YOUR CONSENT WAS AN IMPORTANT **PART** OF THESE MAGICS, AND IT STILL IS. SO YOU GET TO **LIVE--**

--AND TO **WATCH--**

--WHILE YOUR CHILDREN **RAPE** THE WORLD.

I WENT BACK INTO THE *REAL* WORLD.

LIKE A *SAILOR* STEPPING ONTO DRY LAND, FEELING IT ROCK AND *SWAY* UNDER ME.

"AND I AWOKE AND *FOUND* ME HERE, ON THE COLD HILL'S SIDE."

IN DENMARK STREET. IN A PUDDLE OF SOMEONE ELSE'S *PISS.*

I *ATE* HERE ONCE.

BUT THAT WAS WITH KIT. AND LITTLE *ADAM* SPILLED A BOTTLE OF WINE OVER THE PAIR OF US.

SO THAT NEVER *HAPPENED.*

THREE *LIFETIMES* YAWNED BEHIND ME. MY OWN PAST LOST IN THE *MIX* SOMEWHERE, BROKEN INTO PIECES AND TOSSED INTO THE WIND.

A CLOCK STRUCK *MIDNIGHT.* THE LONG *DAY* WAS OFFICIALLY OVER.

BUT THE *WAR*--

OH, THE WAR WAS JUST *BEGINNING.*

END

190

WHERE HORROR, DARK MAGIC,
AND BAD LUCK MEET,
JOHN CONSTANTINE IS NEVER FAR AWAY.

JOHN CONSTANTINE HELLBLAZER

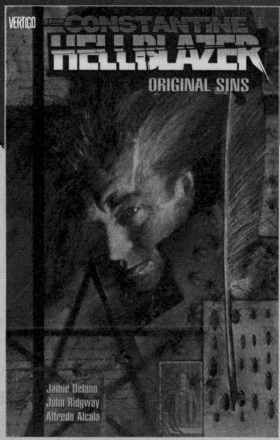

JOHN CONSTANTINE HELLBLAZER
ORIGINAL SINS

The legendary anti-hero and his journeys
through Hell and back are chronicled
in these hair-raising VERTIGO volumes:

ORIGINAL SINS
DANGEROUS HABITS
FEAR AND LOATHING
TAINTED LOVE
DAMNATION'S FLAME
RAKE AT THE GATES OF HELL
SON OF MAN
HAUNTED
SETTING SUN
HARD TIME
GOOD INTENTIONS
FREEZES OVER
HIGHWATER
RARE CUTS
ALL HIS ENGINES
RED SEPULCHRE
BLACK FLOWERS
STARING AT THE WALL

Jamie Delano
John Ridgway
Alfredo Alcala

FEAR and LOATHING
Garth Ennis • Steve Dillon
Introduction by Warren Ellis

HAUNTED
Warren Ellis
John Higgins

BLACK FLOWERS
Mike Carey
Marcelo Frusin
Lee Bermejo
Jock

ALL TITLES ARE SUGGESTED FOR MATURE READERS.

SEARCH THE GRAPHIC NOVELS SECTION OF
www.VERTIGOCOMICS.com

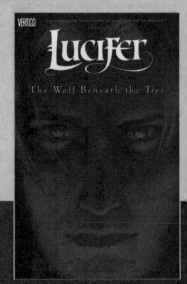